The Feathered Serpent

D0755725

Other 'Be A Detective Mystery Stories'
available in Armada

IMPRIMÉ EN FRANCE

NANCY DREW® AND THE HARDY BOYS®
Be A Detective Mystery Stories ™

The Feathered Serpent

Carolyn Keene and
Franklin W. Dixon

Illustrated by Paul Frame

Armada

First published in the U.S.A.
in 1984 by Wanderer Books,
a division of Simon & Schuster, Inc.
First published in the U.K. in Armada
in 1985 by Fontana Paperbacks,
8 Grafton Street, London W1X 3LA.

© 1984 Stratemeyer Syndicate

'Nancy Drew', 'The Hardy Boys'
and 'Be A Detective Mystery Stories'
are trademarks of the Stratemeyer Syndicate,
registered in the United States
Patent and Trademark Office.

Made and printed for
William Collins Sons & Co. Ltd, Glasgow

Conditions of Sale
This book is sold subject to the condition
that it shall not, by way of trade or otherwise,
be lent, re-sold, hired out or otherwise circulated
without the publisher's prior consent in any form of
binding or cover other than that in which it is
published and without a similar condition
including this condition being imposed
on the subsequent purchaser.

Dear Fans,

Since so many of you have written to us saying how much you want to be detectives like Nancy Drew and The Hardy Boys, we figured out a way. Of course, we had to put our heads together to create mysteries that were so baffling they needed help from everyone including Nancy, Frank, Joe, and you!

In these exciting new BE A DETECTIVE MYSTERY STORIES you'll be part of a great team of amateur sleuths following clues and wily suspects. At every turn you'll have a chance to pick a different trail filled with adventure that may lead to danger, surprise, or an amazing discovery!

The choices are all yours—see how many there are and have fun!

C.K. and F.W.D.

"I'm worried about Nancy," Frank Hardy said to his younger brother Joe as the two scanned the skies from the passenger terminal at Bayport Airport.

Joe nodded his blond head and peered up at the thick overcast of clouds. "She's late," he agreed. "But if she were in trouble, she'd radio for help." He smiled. "Besides, Nancy Drew knows how to take care of herself. Even at 10,000 feet."

Frank glanced out the window. "I guess you're right," he said. "But I'd feel a lot better if her plane were on the ground instead of above those clouds."

Joe headed for a soda machine across the lobby. "Me, too. I want to hear what she thinks about the smuggling scheme Dad's client, Mr. Salazar, believes he's uncovered."

Frank joined Joe at the machine. "You mean *presumed* smuggling scheme," he said with a private detective's tone of skepticism in his voice.

The Hardy brothers, sons of the world-famous investigator, Fenton Hardy, mulled over the thin leads of the case their father had asked them to help unravel.

Turn to page 2.

"Dad's not certain that anything is being smuggled," Frank pointed out. "All he has to go on is Mr. Salazar's suspicion."

Joe nodded. "That's why he went to Mexico," he said. "If anyone down there is smuggling through Salazar's company, Dad'll smoke 'em out."

"And our job is to investigate at this end," Frank declared. He glanced at the dark clouds that filled the sky like dirty wads of cotton. His face was grim. "But what bothers me right now is Nancy. Where could she be?"

If you think Nancy's in danger, turn to page 3.
If you think Nancy's safe, turn to page 4.
If you think Nancy's safe, and you want to stay with Frank and Joe, turn to page 6.
If you'd like Nancy to arrive right away, turn to page 13.

The sharp crackle of the airport loudspeaker filled the room. "Will the airport manager report to the tower immediately?" an anxious voice asked. "There is an emergency. Repeat. Mr. Davis, please report to the tower at once. *Emergency!*"

Just before the speaker went dead, someone else could be heard in the background. It was the voice of a girl whose plane was in distress.

"My instruments are out," she said. "I'm flying blind! But I *should* be making my regular approach over the bay."

Frank and Joe stared at each other. "*Nancy!*" they exclaimed in unison.

To go directly to Nancy, turn to page 5.
To stay with Frank and Joe, turn to page 10.

Nancy banked her bright red plane and began a controlled descent. It'll be just super to work on a case with the Hardys again, she thought as she skillfully piloted the plane through the clouds. I hope they weren't worried because that headwind slowed me down.

Soon Bayport Airport appeared directly ahead of the spinning prop. As Nancy prepared to land, she reviewed the telephone conversation she'd had with Frank and Joe the night before. Mr. Salazar thinks his company is being used to smuggle something out of Mexico, she recalled. But what it is and who is behind it—that is the mystery.

A short while later, the three young friends greeted each other happily, then walked across the airport parking lot toward the Hardys' yellow sports sedan. They chatted about old times at first, but then talked about their new case.

"There are two mysteries as I see it," Nancy said. "One is, *who* is doing the smuggling and, two, *what* is being smuggled?"

"There's something you left out, Nancy," Joe said. "And that is, there may not be even *be* any smuggling."

When they reached the car, Frank suddenly grabbed Joe by the arm, "Look!" he exclaimed.

If you want to know what Frank saw, turn to page 7.
If you want to see what Nancy saw, turn to page 11.

Nancy scanned the thick clouds beneath her small red plane. Somewhere below lay Bayport Airport. But where? she asked herself, as she glanced at her navigation instruments.

Then, without warning, the engine began to sputter. Nancy's eyes darted to the fuel gauge. It read half full, but the sound told her otherwise. With a final, chilling gasp, the engine stopped cold, and the propeller jerked to a sudden halt. Nancy tightened her grip on the wheel. I'm a glider now, she thought. If Bayport isn't directly under these clouds, I'm still over the bay! The fear of a crash in the water made her shudder. "And nobody knows where I am," she said aloud. "Not even me!"

If you think Nancy's over Bayport, turn to page 16.
If you fear she's over the bay, turn to page 30.

Joe dropped a coin into the soda machine. Instantly a piercing wail split the air. *Whoop, whoop*. It came from the soft-drink dispenser. A flashing red light atop the machine began to blink. Joe leaped backward in surprise.

"It looks like you hit the jackpot," Frank said with a laugh. "But no soda."

Before the young detectives could say another word, a uniformed security guard appeared on the run. "Don't either of you move," he ordered as he grabbed Joe firmly by the arm. "You're under arrest."

Joe and Frank were dumbfounded. "Arrest?" Frank asked. "What for?"

"For using a counterfeit coin in this machine," the guard replied. Then he opened the machine with a key. "All I need is the evidence."

"This must be a mistake!" Joe protested, showing the officer a handful of coins. "Why would I use a slug if I have plenty of real coins?"

An airport official approached. "Let those young men go, officer," he said. "Those are Fenton Hardy's sons. I'm sure there's an explanation."

Turn to page 20.

The three sleuths stared at a perfectly round hole in the driver's side window of the yellow sports car. "A bullet hole!" Frank gasped.

Instinctively the young detectives huddled for cover next to the car in case the person who fired the shot was still around.

"It may have been a stray shot," Joe suggested when there was no sign of movement near them and they felt safe enough to stand up again.

"Or a warning," Frank said. "It's dead center in the window. That's too precise for a random shot."

Turn to page 9.

Nancy glanced around the nearly empty parking lot. "If it's a warning to us," she said, "who made it? And why?" Her eyes lighted on a low hedge fifty yards from the car. "The hole was made by a small-caliber bullet," she went on. "A pistol would have just enough power to reach the car from that hedge. Come on, let's check it out."

She ran off, and when the boys joined her, she was already studying the soft earth behind the hedge. She picked up a small object and examined it with the magnifying glass she always carried. "The empty cartridge," Nancy exclaimed. Then she bent down again and retrieved a crumpled tissue. "Ah," she said. "This tells me something about the person who fired the shot."

If you want to hear Nancy's clue, turn to page 14.
If you want to investigate further, turn to page 15.

Frank and Joe ran to the control tower to get Nancy's position. Then they drove to the boat house where they kept their motorboat, the *Sleuth*.

Frank started its mighty engine and headed out to the bay while Joe was reviewing the charts. "She's about a mile offshore," he said. "If we're lucky, we'll be able to sight her."

"Keep a lookout with those binoculars," Frank said. "If she landed on the plane's belly, it'll float. But if it flipped . . . " Neither of them dared think of the consequences of a crash.

The *Sleuth* leaped over the waves as if it had wings. A speck danced on a distant wave. Joe pressed his binoculars to his eyes. "It's red!" he shouted. "I think it's Nancy's plane." Then his mouth dropped open. "But it's *empty!*"

Suddenly he caught a glimmer of titian-red hair in the water. It was Nancy, bobbing in the sea next to the sinking plane.

Joe stripped off his shirt and pants and kicked off his shoes as Frank steered the *Sleuth* as close to the wreck as he dared. Then he dived into the water.

"Thanks for fishing me out!" Nancy said with a grateful grin as Frank helped her into the boat. Clenched in her fist was something that would add to the mystery.

"What's that?" Joe asked curiously while he reached into a locker for two towels.

Turn to page 12.

While the Hardys were watching a cat stroll leisurely across the roof of their car, Nancy had noticed a slip of paper stuck under the windshield blade. She pulled it out and read it aloud. "H-49 9:45 HELP," she said. "What do you think it means?"

"Somebody needs help—that's clear," Joe said.

"And 9:45 is only five minutes from now, so the writer must be nearby to expect us to meet him," Frank said. "But the H-49. I don't know."

Nancy was thinking hard while she listened to the boys' deductions. "Nearby? Hmm?" she said. Her face brightened. "I think I have the answer. Follow me."

Soon the three investigators stood in the shadow of a giant airplane hangar. Like all the buildings at Bayport Airport, it had a large identifying number painted on its side.

"H-49" Frank said, checking the building number against the one on the mysterious note. "This is it."

"We'd better split up," Joe suggested. "It could be a trap."

Nancy and Frank agreed.

To investigate with Joe, turn to page 46.
To follow Nancy, turn to page 48.
To stay with Frank, turn to page 53.

But before Nancy could answer him, Frank shouted loudly:

"Someone's prowling around our boathouse!" Frank quickly turned the *Sleuth* around and headed back. Bubbles were rising from the water near their dock and popped to the surface like tiny, hollow jellyfish.

"A scuba diver," Nancy said. "Could it be someone connected with the smuggling scheme? Or my plane crash?" Still in her hand was a ball of soft white material that she had removed from the wreck.

Then a black hood covered by a thick glass mask broke the surface. "He's huge," Nancy gasped.

"Don't let him hear you say that," Frank said with a grin.

The Hardys' best friend Chet Morton climbed aboard the *Sleuth*. "Uh, oh," he muttered, as he took off his mask. "Nancy's here. Something tells me I've swum into the middle of a mystery."

The investigators nodded grimly. "That you have," Joe said. "Why don't you come over to the house with us and we'll tell you all about it."

Half an hour later, the Hardys and their friends were sitting in the boys' crime lab over their garage.

Turn to page 24.

As Frank and Joe scanned the clouds, a large hole broke in the overcast sky. A small red speck glided toward the airport.

"There she is," Joe said with a sigh of relief. "Let's go outside and meet her."

"We were worried about you," Frank said to Nancy as she stepped out of her plane.

The girl grinned. "I knew exactly where I was every minute," she said. "But I have to admit I wasn't sure if Bayport knew where it was supposed to be."

The three friends laughed as they rode to the big frame house on Elm Street where Frank and Joe lived.

Aunt Gertrude, their father's sister, met them at the door with a picnic basket of freshly fried chicken, hot biscuits, and a cold pitcher of lemonade.

"It's so nice to see you again, Nancy," Miss Hardy said and hugged the girl. Then, to the boys, she added, "There's a message from your father on the telephone recorder."

Turn to page 39.

Frank and Joe grinned broadly. They knew Nancy was an excellent detective. "Well," Frank said, "go ahead!"

Nancy held the tissue first beneath Frank's nose, then Joe's. Each sniffed it carefully.

"It was a woman, don't you agree?" she deduced.

The boys nodded. They had detected the faint scent of perfume on the tissue. "Obviously the lady kept the tissue in her purse long enough for it to absorb the smell of her perfume," Frank said.

Joe was on his knees, staring at the ground. "Not only does she carry a purse," he said, "but she wears high-heeled shoes, weighs about 100 pounds, and is between five feet and five feet three inches tall."

"How'd you figure that out so quickly?" Frank asked his brother.

To hear Joe's deductions, turn to page 17.

Frank and Joe were amazed that Nancy had spotted a clue already. "What about who fired the gun?" Joe asked.

"The cartridge is still warm," Nancy said, "so the shot was fired only moments ago. That means whoever did it is nearby."

As she spoke, Joe spotted someone walking briskly away from the parking lot. He had black hair and was wearing a red shirt and a green baseball cap. The man glanced over his shoulder, then started to run. "That must be him!" Joe cried.

Immediately the three gave chase. They raced in pursuit of their suspect, who rounded a corner. When the young detectives dashed around the same bend, the man was gone! They searched the area, but he had escaped! Disappointed, they reviewed the observations they'd made of the stranger, putting together an accurate description, but without knowing what his face looked like.

After they finished comparing notes, Nancy said suddenly, "I think I know where we can find him."

"Where?" Joe asked.

"He's bound to drive out the airport exit," Nancy explained. "If we could only get there before him . . ."

Turn to page 26.

The tiny plane continued to descend toward the clouds. Nancy remained calm. Just as a skilled pilot would do, she reviewed the emergency procedures. There's been a short circuit in the electrical system, she thought. That accounts for the navigation instruments going out. She tapped the glass on the front of the fuel gauge. The tiny arrow wiggled, but it continued to read *half full*.

Suddenly the plane was enveloped in clouds. Without instruments to guide her, Nancy could go into a fatal spin at any moment! She avoided looking out the window to prevent vertigo—the dizziness that keeps people from recognizing up from down. "I've got to concentrate on remaining level," she said out loud. "But I also have to restart the engine. The fuel tank may be blocked."

She carefully rocked the wings back and forth. If there was any fuel in the tank it would undo the blockage. She flipped the key. The engine turned over. It coughed and sputtered. Suddenly it roared to life, and the instruments were working again. There's a loose wire somewhere that caused it all, Nancy deduced as the plane broke through the clouds.

Turn to page 13.

Joe bent down slightly so he could peer through a small opening in the hedge where a branch had been broken. Then he pointed to the ground.

"This is where she stood," he said. "Those are her heelprints." He indicated two small holes punched into the soil. "High heels, right?"

"Yes," Nancy said. "And your estimate of her weight is good. If she weighed more, the holes would be much deeper."

"Also, the hole she made to shoot through the hedge is just about right for a five-footer to sight through," Frank added.

After making sure they'd found all the clues by the hedge, the three returned to the car.

"How many people knew I was flying to Bayport to help with the investigation?" Nancy asked.

"Five," Frank said. "Dad, Joe, and I, of course. So did Salazar. That makes four."

Joe and Nancy waited but Frank was silent.

"Well?" Nancy said. "Who was the fifth one?"

"The person who fired the warning shot," Frank said. "And that's who we have to find next."

"Where do we start?" Nancy asked.

"Well, since we have no idea where the lady with the gun went, we might as well go to New York and check out Salazar's office," Frank replied.

Turn to the next page.

Frank drove the yellow sports sedan while Nancy and Joe discussed the case. Finally they were approaching the dramatic skyline of New York City, which sparkled in the distance like a range of man-made mountains.

"Salazar is in Mexico with Dad," Joe said. "But my guess is somebody in his office knows we're investigating the case at this end."

"And that may be the person who fired the warning shot," Nancy declared.

"I agree," Frank said as he entered the Lincoln Tunnel.

"But something is troubling me," Nancy said.

"What's that," Joe asked.

"We know it was a woman," Nancy replied. "But what was her motive? Does she want us to stop the investigation? Or was she warning us that somebody else wants it stopped?"

Turn to page 22.

"The warehouse door is open," Frank said to Joe as they cautiously made their way around the building. "Let's go in."

Quietly the Hardy brothers slipped into the large building. It was piled high with wooden shipping crates marked HECHO EN MEXICO.

"Made in Mexico," Joe said. "These boxes are big enough to hold bicycles."

Frank was looking at a clipboard hanging on a wall. "I think I've found a clue," he said. He showed Joe the paper attached to the clipboard. It was a shipping list. At the bottom were the initials S.I.C. "Is this our mysterious friend?"

Just then a connecting door from the office in front opened and a young man entered. Another man was shouting after him. "If I catch you poking around any more, you're fired!"

Joe and Frank nodded to each other. "I think he's our lead," Joe whispered.

A moment later, the young man saw the boys. He quickly closed the door. "Joe and Frank Hardy?" he whispered. "Then the rumor was true. You *are* investigating Salazar's company! I wasn't sure, but I tried to signal you with a coin containing my uncle's initials and—"

Joe flipped the Mexican coin to the young man. "I know," he said. "I almost got arrested for using it."

Turn to page 25.

The security guard relaxed his grip on Joe. "It better be a good one," he said. He extended his other hand to the official. In it was the coin the boy had put into the machine. "This is a fake!"

Frank and Joe stared at the money. It was old and worn, and looked like foreign currency.

"May I see it, sir?" Frank asked politely. He took the coin from the security guard and turned it slowly in the light. "My brother may be guilty of putting this into the machine," he went on, "but I assure you it was an honest mistake. This is a Mexican coin, and if my detective instincts are right, it has something to do with a case we're working on right now."

A quick explanation to the airport official was enough to make him realize that he'd stepped into the middle of a Hardy investigation. He apologized to Frank and Joe. "I figured there was a reason," he said. "I know your fine reputations well enough to realize you'd never do a thing like this. Good luck on your case."

"That was close," Joe said to Frank after the two men had left.

His brother turned the strange coin over and over in his hand. "How'd you get this?" he asked.

Joe looked blank. "I have no idea."

Turn to the next page.

Just then Nancy Drew entered the waiting room and hurried toward the boys.

"Sorry I'm late!" she cried out. "I had a little trouble landing, but it went all right."

Frank and Joe greeted their friend warmly. "We were worried about you," Frank said. "But you're just in time. If you'd arrived a moment earlier, you'd have been arrested."

"What!"

The Hardys quickly explained what had happened, and Frank showed Nancy the strange coin.

"I bet it's a clue," she said. "But what does it mean?"

"We don't even know how Joe got it," Frank said.

Nancy took out her magnifying glass for a closer examination. She looked at the coin for quite a while, then she said, "I think I found something!"

She held the coin and the glass so the boys could see. Etched in the dark surface of the metal were the letters S.I.C. "It looks as if someone did it with a pin," she concluded.

"It could stand for Salazar Importing Company!" Frank exclaimed.

"Maybe," Nancy said.

The three young people went out of the terminal to the parking lot, where they piled into the Hardys' yellow sports sedan with Joe behind the wheel.

Turn to page 49.

Frank drove through the heavy New York City traffic. While he concentrated on getting safely to Salazar's warehouse, Joe and Nancy developed a plan.

"We should go undercover," Nancy suggested.

"I agree," Joe said. "Anyone who would fire a gun illegally is dangerous to us."

Frank nodded as he parked the car. "Salazar's office is around the corner," he said. "Let's go."

Soon the investigators approached the building housing Salazar's import business, which was in a rundown neighborhood. It was a one-story warehouse with offices in the front.

Nancy smoothed her hair and adjusted her clothes. "I'll go to the office," she said. "You two can look around in back for anything suspicious."

To follow Nancy, turn to page 27.

The next morning the investigators, dressed for a day as tourists in New York City, casually approached the Totten Art Gallery on Fifth Avenue and entered the elegant shop. They told the receptionist who they were; Mr. Totten appeared to greet them himself shortly afterward. "Nancy Drew and the Hardy brothers," he said. "What an honor."

"Nancy is visiting us from River Heights," Joe said, "and we came to New York City for some shopping."

"Oh, please make yourselves at home in my little shop," R. Burton Totten said as he gestured at the fabulous art pieces for sale in his exclusive gallery.

The boys engaged Totten in light conversation as Nancy, pretending to browse, investigated the rear of the gallery. When no one was looking, she slipped into Totten's office. On his desk was a crude Mexican pot, hardly the kind of piece a fine art dealer would carry. She studied it closely. When she inspected the underside, she saw a large "X" that had been initialed when the clay was still wet.

Later, back on the street, she reported her finding to the boys. "He receives something that's being smuggled in pots marked by an 'X,' " she concluded.

"But what is it?" Joe asked.

"That's what we have to find out," Frank said. "Tonight!"

Turn to page 31.

"Dad's not convinced that anything is being smuggled," Joe explained to Nancy and Chet. "He's going to radio us tonight."

Chet was studying the white material that Nancy had taken from her downed plane. "It's definitely plastic foam," he said. "The kind that's used to pack fragile objects for shipping. It's molded around the item like this cookie dough is molded around the chocolate chips." Chet popped his demonstration cookie into his mouth. "Where did you find this stuff, Nancy?"

"In my fuel tanks," the girl said grimly. "Someone filled them half full of foam so they'd only hold a half tank of gas."

"Then it was sabotage," Frank said.

"But is there any connection with the suspected smuggling scheme?" Joe asked.

"A trip to Salazar's warehouse might turn up the answer to that," Nancy said.

Soon the four friends were on their way to New York City.

Turn to page 38.

"I'm Ricardo Salazar," the young man said. "Ernesto Salazar is my father. He hired your father to investigate the smuggling."

"Then there *is* a smuggling operation?" Joe asked.

Ricardo shrugged his shoulders. "We're not sure. That's the problem. We think my uncle Sergio Iodello-Casate, who was hollering at me just now, is smuggling something from Mexico because he is suddenly very rich. But we don't know what it is. Each day I go through every crate that comes in, and I have found nothing."

Just then the door to the office flew open and a fat man bounded out. His face was beet red and he pointed a gun at the young people. "I warned you," he screamed at Ricardo. "I know these two. They are the Hardy brothers. You and your father! You have hired detectives to uncover something but it is too late!"

A heavily muscled man was behind the suspected smuggler. He immediately grabbed Frank and Joe while the fat man grabbed Ricardo. "You will regret nosing in my affairs, nephew," Sergio said. He turned to Frank and Joe. "And you will regret right along with him. Put them in a box, Pedro," he ordered his accomplice.

Turn to page 40.

A short while later, the three young detectives sat in the Hardys' yellow sports sedan by the airport exit observing every vehicle leaving the area. At last Joe spotted a small pickup truck. "There he is," he shouted. "Black hair, red shirt, green baseball cap . . ."

Frank started the car and soon the investigators were tailing the man, who drove rather slowly. Frank had to be careful not to get too close.

Nancy was quiet. "Something bothers me about this guy," she said at last. "It's almost as if he *wants* us to follow him."

"I was thinking the same thing," Joe said. "It's as if he's doing everything in his power to catch our attention. The warning shot. Hanging around until we spotted him. Wearing clothes anybody could pick out of a crowd . . ."

"And now going slow enough so we can't possibly lose him," Frank added. "My guess is he's leading us into a trap."

"*Thinks* he is," Nancy said.

The others nodded, and together they prepared a plan. "We'll have the police cover us," Frank said and called the authorities on his CB radio.

Turn to page 36.

Nancy took a deep breath and entered the office of Salazar Importing Company. Two people sat at desks behind a counter, a burly man with short gray hair and a woman who was bent over her work. Nancy's eyes darted around the room, absorbing every detail.

"Whaddya want?" the man asked gruffly.

"I'm a recent graduate of Bale's Secretarial School in Boston," Nancy said. "I'd like to apply for a job."

"We ain't hiring," the man told her curtly.

Nancy needed more time to look for clues. "May I fill out an application?" she asked.

"No point to it," the man said.

The woman at the desk hadn't moved. Nancy wanted to get a good look at her before leaving. "Oh!" she exclaimed. "I've got something in my eye. May I borrow a tissue from you?"

The woman, who was very tall, stood up. She dug in her purse and handed Nancy a white tissue.

The young detective daubed her eye while quietly sniffing the tissue. There was no trace of perfume. As she was about to leave, a door at the rear opened, and a draft of air cut through the room. The perfume! Nancy thought. Then the door slammed. Whoever had opened it was gone!

Turn to the next page.

As Nancy turned to leave the office, the phone rang. The man answered it. He glared briefly at the girl, then slammed down the receiver. "Maybe we are lookin' for a new secretary after all," he said.

Nancy sensed danger. "I'll send my résumé," she told him and headed for the door.

"Stop her, Ella!" the man shouted.

Nancy ran, but the tall woman intercepted her and grabbed her by the arm. The young detective struggled fiercely, but Ella was much larger than she. If I use karate, the man will join her, the girl thought. And I can't overpower them both.

Just then the man grabbed Nancy's free arm. "You've got some explaining to do—*Nancy Drew!*" he hissed.

Nancy's mind was working fast. Whoever made that call is the person we're looking for, she thought.

"Tie her up," the man said. "We'll dump her into the East River."

Nancy shuddered. She knew Frank and Joe were nearby. But did they know she was in danger?

If you think Frank and Joe can help, turn to page 35.
If you suspect the worst, turn to page 33.

Nancy's eyes filled with horror as her tiny plane dropped out of the clouds into clear air. Bayport was nowhere in sight! Only the vast expanse of Barmet Bay filled the horizon.

"Mayday! Mayday! Mayday!" she called on the emergency radio channel. "This is Nancy Drew. I'm out of fuel. Last known position was ten miles east of Bayport. Mayday!"

Will someone hear me before I crash? Nancy wondered as the falling plane swooped nearer and nearer to the cold gray water below.

She snugged her seat belt tightly around her waist as the first icy fingers of the bay reached up to grab the airplane's thin skin. Then she pulled back sharply on the stick so the craft would flop belly first into the water.

With the sound of exploding thunder, she smashed into the frigid bay.

Turn to page 37.

Once again, Sylvia Indo-Cruz let the investigators into the empty warehouse that night. Using flashlights, they searched the scores of crates which had arrived that day. At last Nancy found something. "Come here," she whispered excitedly. "This may be it." She held up a pot similar to the one she'd seen in Totten's gallery. On its bottom was an "X." The other pots in the shipment had no such mark.

"Whatever is being smuggled is inside," Joe said, reaching into the dark cavity. But his hand came out empty! A puzzled expression creased his face. "Nothing's there!"

Frank took the pot from his brother. He tapped it gently around the sides. A steady *pink, pink, pink* sounded each time his finger struck the pot. Then, *plunk!* Nancy and the boys stared at the little container as if they could see through it. "Something's baked in the clay!" Frank declared.

Just then, the sound of a car could be heard outside. The young detectives hastily replaced the pot, then hurried to hide. A moment later, the warehouse door opened and R. Burton Totten entered. He poked around the new shipment of jars until he found the one he was looking for, then departed.

"We have to visit his shop again," Nancy said.

Turn to the next page.

Shortly afterward, the group had climbed onto the roof of the one-story gallery. They gasped as they watched Totten through the skylight. He put the clay pot on his desk, then struck it a blow with a small hammer, shattering it into hundreds of small shards! And when the rough clay had fallen away, an exquisitely crafted feather made of the finest gold lay on the rubble. It was as delicate as an insect's wing and as fine as a cobweb.

"What a magnificent piece," Nancy whispered.

The Hardys were awed. "It has to be a Mexican national treasure," Frank said. "We've got to call Dad right away so he'll know what's being smuggled. That way he can catch the crooks at that end while we close in on Totten."

The young people contacted Mr. Hardy from a pay phone. "It's just the lead I need," he said. "Don't move in on Totten until I get back to you."

There was nothing else the three detectives could do but return home and wait.

Turn to page 44.

The rear office door opened again and the familiar perfume floated through the air. Nancy was curious to see who wore it, but to her surprise, Frank and Joe entered the office, with their hands up in the air!

Behind them was a small woman with a gun aimed at the two boys.

"Who are they, Lorraine?" the burly man asked.

"The Hardy boys," the woman replied. "And that's Nancy Drew, just like I told you on the phone. I guess my warning shot wasn't enough for them. Tie them all up. Now they'll know we mean business."

"Smuggling business," Nancy accused her.

"Ha, ha, ha," Lorraine laughed sarcastically. "That's what Salazar thinks."

"It's not smuggling, Nancy," Frank said. "It's hijacking. I didn't have a chance to tell you because she caught us."

"You're a pretty good detective," the woman scoffed.

"And you're a pretty poor thief," Joe said. "We found this in the warehouse." In his raised right hand he waved a stained stencil that was marked *Hecho en Mexico*. "They've been hijacking trucks with clothing made right here in New York and repacking the merchandise as if it came from Mexico. They paint *Made in Mexico* on the crates and ship them to unsuspecting stores. Salazar became suspicious. He knew he hadn't imported the clothing."

Turn to the next page.

"You're all too smart for your own good," Lorraine shouted. "That's why we're going to get rid of you."

The man got up and walked toward the boys. But Nancy and the Hardys had been signaling to one another and were ready for the next move.

"Now!" Nancy shouted. With that, she leaped at Ella. At the same moment, Joe lunged for the man and Frank kicked the gun from Lorraine's hand.

With flashing fists and silent karate chops, the three young detectives quickly subdued the startled gang. In minutes the criminals were prisoners and the sleuths their guards.

Frank dialed the phone as Nancy and Joe kept a cautious eye on the three captives. "The New York City Police will be happy to hear about you," he said.

"And Salazar will be even happier to know his warehouse has been exterminated of rats," Joe added.

END

Joe looked nervously at his watch. "Nancy's been in there too long, if you ask me," he said. "Let's check on her."

Frank grabbed his younger brother by the arm. "We won't have to," he said. "There she is now."

Nancy was being dragged to a black sedan parked behind Salazar's warehouse by a burly man and a tall woman. A third person, a small, dark-haired woman, was the obvious boss. "We'll get rid of her before those nosy Hardy brothers know we've got her," she said.

"That's what *she* thinks," Frank said grimly. "We'll follow them. Maybe we'll be able to uncover the smuggling scheme."

Joe was already on the way to their car.

Turn to page 41.

After a while, the pickup truck pulled into an abandoned farm several miles from the airport. The driver got out and entered a large, dilapidated barn.

Frank followed him into the farmyard. "We have to let him think we've fallen into his trap," he declared.

"Then he'll fall into ours," Joe said with a wink and reported their location to the police over the CB radio.

"Let's go into the barn and talk to the driver," Nancy suggested. "We can pretend we're lost."

"Good idea," Frank said.

The young detectives walked up to the old building, hesitated a moment, then opened the door and entered. The man stood inside.

"Excuse me. We got lost and were wondering if you could direct us," Frank spoke up.

The man laughed. "I think I can do more than that," he said. He pulled off his cap and a black wig, then rubbed makeup from his face. "I can even tell you what this is all about," he added.

"Sam!" the Hardys and Nancy cried in unison. "Sam Radley!"

The stranger was indeed Fenton Hardy's able assistant.

Turn to page 42.

Nancy unsnapped the safety belt as the rising water reached her seat. The bright young detective faced a life-or-death situation and she knew it. With a thrust of her shoulder, she forced the door open. Water gushed in, but with cool aplomb, Nancy plunged into the bay.

She climbed on the wing of the half-submerged plane. The air in the fuel tanks will keep it afloat for a while, she thought. But how long?

Always curious, even in danger, Nancy investigated the cause of the crash—the strange fact that she had run out of gas unexpectedly. She carefully crawled to the wing tank and unscrewed the cap. She put her eye to the opening and peered inside. She was stunned by what she saw and her hand flew into the tank. When she pulled it out, she clutched a fistful of white plastic foam.

"Sabotage!" she exclaimed. "Someone filled the tanks half full of plastic foam so they would read full when they really weren't!"

The sound of a distant engine caught Nancy's attention, and soon a sleek motorboat came into sight. Frank and Joe! she thought. I knew they wouldn't let me down.

A moment later, the Hardy boys' *Sleuth* pulled alongside her. As Nancy stepped aboard, the plane upended and sank beneath the waves.

Turn to page 54.

"Salazar's warehouse will be closed when we get there," Frank said. "That'll give us time to investigate without being noticed. *If* the place isn't being guarded."

Chet gulped. He enjoyed working on a case with his friends, but he preferred the security of a science lab to prowling around dark alleys. "I felt safer searching for sea urchins off your dock," he said.

Nancy gave him a disapproving look. "Well, you weren't," she said. "Diving alone is dangerous!"

Chet's chin dropped to his chest. "I know," he said. "I'll never do it again."

The warehouse was abandoned when the young people arrived. "It's the perfect place for some kind of secret operation," Joe said after examining the place.

While Chet stood guard with instructions to whistle three times if anyone suspicious came near, Nancy and Joe slipped around to the rear of the building while Frank investigated the front.

To investigate with Frank, turn to page 43.
To go with Nancy and Joe, turn to page 45.

Nancy, Frank, and Joe hovered over the answering machine as Fenton Hardy's voice played from a tape made an hour earlier. "There has been a new development in my investigaton of Salazar's importing company," the message said. "Come to Mexico City at once. I'll have a taxi meet you at the Angel on Avenida Reforma."

"We can catch the next flight if we hurry," Joe said.

"Good thing I haven't had time to unpack." Nancy smiled.

"Just give us a minute to get a few things," Joe told her. "Then we'll go."

Frank grinned. "Now I know why Aunt Gertrude greeted us with a picnic basket."

To follow the sleuths to Mexico, turn to page 60.
If you have doubts about the taped message, turn to page 64.

The three captives were tied securely and placed into a large packing crate. Pedro went to look in a pile of dismantled boxes for a lid, but Sergio stopped him.

"Not those, you fool!" he hissed.

The muscular man found another lid and nailed it tightly over the boys. They could hear Sergio's voice as the warehouse door was opened. "Bring in the truck. We'll dump the box in the middle of the harbor, and that'll be the end of those snoopers."

Nancy watched from behind a nearby bush as Pedro backed a pickup truck into the warehouse and the two men loaded the crate in the back. Then Pedro climbed behind the wheel.

"When you come back," Sergio told him, "load up the dismantled boxes and deliver them."

There's something strange about those old crates, Nancy thought. I have to look into it. But first I'd better save the Hardys and that young man.

Turn to page 55.

Nancy had been pushed into the back seat of the black sedan. The small woman moved in next to her, while the other two sat in front.

Nancy's only hope was that Frank and Joe had seen her and would call the police. But she set aside her concerns for her personal safety to relentlessly pursue the case she'd come to investigate. "It was you who fired the bullet into the Hardys' car, wasn't it?" she asked the woman beside her.

"It was a warning to those boys to stay away. Once we found out Mr. Hardy got involved, we knew his sons would be sticking their noses into our business as well. So I went to Bayport and staked out their house. After they went to the airport, I shot into the window. I should have punctured all their tires, instead! But it doesn't matter. They'll be busy looking for you now. That'll keep them out of trouble."

The car stopped under a bridge, and the man roughly pulled Nancy out. "What shall I do with her, Lorraine?" he asked the woman.

"You know what to do," Lorraine replied and turned away.

Turn to page 99.

Sam quickly explained the reason for the deception.

"Your father went to Mexico thinking he was investigating a smuggling operation," the man said. "He soon learned that a foreign country was using Salazar's company to transfer high-technology computer parts that were illegally purchased in this country."

"You mean something like micro-chips?" Joe asked.

"Right," Sam said. "Now, your father felt that if the foreign buyers learned their scheme was uncovered, they would stop it before we had enough facts to prosecute them. Sure enough, they suspected Salazar's company was being checked out, and the moment your dad learned about their suspicions, he stopped his investigation."

"And it was important that we stop, too, or the foreign buyers would know for sure they'd been discovered," Nancy said.

"Precisely," Sam said. "I knew there were foreign agents following Frank and Joe when they went to the airport to get you, Nancy."

"So you devised the trick to have us follow you, letting them think we were after something else!" Frank said.

"That's right. The trouble is, the agents are out there now, watching our every move!"

Turn to page 50.

Frank circled the entire building, peering in one window after another. Then he rejoined the others. "There's nobody here," he said.

"That's just fine by me," Chet said. "Now, if only *we* weren't here—"

His words were interrupted by the approach of a large black sedan. There was no time to hide before the car was upon them. It screeched to a halt and two men with guns leaped out. "Grab them, Sergio," one said.

"See what I mean?" Chet gulped.

As the criminal guarded the surprised investigators, his accomplice tied their hands. "Now get into the car," he hissed when he was finished.

The car drove out of New York City in the direction of Bayport. "I figured you'd be nosing around here," Sergio said. "I guess you didn't realize I was serious when I sabotaged your plane, Miss Drew. Well, now you know. But it's too late!"

Turn to page 57.

The next day Fenton Hardy called home from Mexico City. "The culprit here is Sylvia Indo-Cruz's brother. He was being blackmailed to smuggle the stolen Feathered Serpent to Totten. He thinks his sister will be deported from the United States if he doesn't do what they demand. They told him that she's not a legal citizen, which is a lie, but he fell for it. Move in on Totten before he gets word that we're aware of his scheme."

The investigators immediately drove back to Totten's Fifth Avenue gallery. He was just going out the front door with a large box in his arms when the three youths confronted him. His head fell dejectedly to his chest. Without a word, he handed the box over to Joe. "My accomplice in Mexico City called me two minutes ago," he said. "He told me that Fenton Hardy broke the case—with your help. I knew you'd be back; I thought I could escape, but it's too late. The Feathered Serpent is in the box. The piece that arrived last night was the final segment. One more day and I would have gotten away with the art crime of the century . . . ."

"But as it is, you've got nothing," Frank said.

"And Mexico will have its national treasure back," Nancy added happily.

END

At the back of the warehouse, Nancy and Joe found a large waste-disposal container resting against the wall facing an alley.

"Garbage investigation may not be very glamorous," Nancy declared, "but many criminals have been caught because their trash gave them away."

She opened the lid and Joe climbed into the trash bin. Suddenly, a shrill whistle split the air, followed by two more. The warning from Chet! A moment later, the rumble of a large truck echoed in the alley. Nancy clambered into the bin with Joe.

"I hope it's not the trash collector," she whispered. But it was!

Frank and Chet had peered around the building and saw their companions climb into the container.

"The truck will haul them away if we don't rescue them," Frank said anxiously. "We can't alert the driver that somebody's in the bin. He'd know that we were poking around, and that would give away our investigation."

"What'll we do?" Chet asked.

"Start running." Frank said. "I'll chase you past the truck. The driver will watch us and that'll give Nancy and Joe a chance to escape."

"It's a good idea except for one thing," Chet said. "I better chase you because if you chase me, you'll catch up too fast!"

Frank grinned. "You're right, Slim. Let's go!"

Turn to page 52.

Joe cautiously entered the giant hangar.

"Pssst!"

He stopped and peered deep into the inky darkness of the huge structure. The ghostly shapes of two large jetliners filled the building.

"Over here," a tense voice called.

Joe moved into the shadows, where a nervous man in a dark green shirt watched him with narrowed, shifting eyes.

"Where are the others?" the man inquired anxiously.

"Who wants to know?" Joe answered, unwilling to reveal too much until he knew more about the uneasy stranger.

"I do," the man said. "I am Ernesto Salazar. I hired your father to investigate smuggling in my company."

"I thought you went to Mexico," Joe said.

"Your dad did, but we decided I should stay," Salazar went on.

Joe relaxed somewhat, but the man's behavior kept his investigator's instincts primed for anything unexpected. "Did you put the note on our car?" he asked.

"Yes," Salazar responded. "My brother Enrico and I are being blackmailed."

Turn to page 62.

The instant Frank and Joe were gone, a burly man stepped from the shadows and grabbed Nancy from behind. He clapped a hand over her mouth before she could scream and dragged her into the darkness of the huge hangar. Then he tied her hands securely and put a gag in her mouth.

"Do exactly as I say," the man ordered, "and you won't get hurt. Now walk to the parking lot as if nothing's wrong. I'll be right next to you every step of the way." He pushed a sharp object into her back.

Nancy did as the man said, knowing it would be foolhardy to resist. As the two crossed the hangar and walked toward the open door, her quick mind recognized her only chance to let Joe and Frank know where she had gone. She staggered as if losing her balance, jumping a few quick steps to the side before recovering. The man stayed right by her side, and they both stepped into a thin spill of oil that lay on the floor. Then they went out into the sunlight.

Turn to page 58.

When Joe stopped at the exit to pay their parking fee, he reached into the change tray of the car. It was empty. He dug in his pocket for money, paid the attendant, then turned toward the highway.

"I think I know how this coin got into your possession," Nancy said and pointed to the change tray on the dashboard.

Frank slapped his knee. "Of course," he said. "We usually have a handful of coins in that dish to pay highway tolls. When we parked at the airport, Joe scooped them up and put them into his pocket."

"I remember," Joe said. "The Mexican coin must have been in the tray! But who put it there?"

"Maybe the driver from Salazar's office who came to pick up Dad," Frank said. "He was standing in the driveway waiting for quite a while."

"Then the coin *is* connected with the case," Nancy said. "It must be a message. One or more people want us to know about them, without giving themselves away. But who?"

"Let's start our investigation with Salazar in New York," Frank decided.

Turn to page 56.

Nancy peeked out of a crack in the side of the barn. Near the farm entrance, mostly concealed by bushes, was a black car.

"You're right," she said. "There are two men watching."

Sam looked concerned. "By the way, I'm sorry I had to put the hole in your car, but time was of the essence and it was the only thing I could think of doing. I'll have it fixed for you. Now we have to figure out the next step. I'm not sure what it should be."

"You don't have a thing to worry about, Sam," Joe said. He checked his watch. "In about five seconds you're going to be arrested."

"What!"

Just then, wailing sirens filled the air. Soon the farmyard was swarming with sheriff's deputies. The foreign agents in the black car watched in awe as Sam Radley, in disguise again, was brought out of the barn in handcuffs and hauled away.

The next day a newspaper article described how the Hardy boys and Nancy Drew had captured a suspect they'd been after "for weeks."

"That should convince the foreign agents we weren't investigating Salazar," Joe said with a chuckle.

"And once their guard is down, Dad will find the evidence needed to put them out of business for good!" Frank added.

END

The next day the New York City newspapers carried a tragic headline: NANCY DREW LOST AT SEA. FENTON HARDY RETURNING TO UNITED STATES FROM MEXICO TO JOIN SEARCH. A picture showed the investigator stepping off an airplane in New York. The story, made up with the help of the police, saddened millions of people. Nancy Drew, even though only a young girl, was a famous detective who was loved by everyone.

"If I didn't know that was Sam Radley disguised as Dad, I'd really believe our father was back here instead of in Mexico waiting for the smugglers to make their move," Joe said.

A secret radio message that night from Fenton Hardy confirmed that the trap had worked. "The smugglers have put a valuable stolen art treasure on flight 485 to New York," the famous investigator said. "Be there when it arrives."

Joe, Frank, Nancy and Chet were at the international airport early the next morning with members of the New York City police. The stolen goods were found and the smuggling operation squelched.

"I think I've had enough excitement for a while," Nancy said later as she boarded a commercial airliner for her flight home. "But if you ever need me to help with another investigation, I'll be ready."

END

The truck driver chuckled as he saw the two youths rush by him. "Kids," he said as Chet shook his fist at the fleeing Frank. "If that chubby fella ever catches the quick one, he'll give him the business for sure."

The minute Joe and Nancy heard the commotion, they leaped out of the container. "Make a break for it," Joe whispered to the girl, and they rushed around the corner of the building.

The four investigators were safely hidden when the truck rumbled away with the trash. The driver never knew what precious cargo he had almost carted off to the dump.

When he was gone, Nancy held out her hand for the others to see. In it was a large chunk of white plastic foam.

"It's the same stuff you got from your fuel tanks!" Chet exclaimed after a quick examination of the material.

Now they knew for certain there was a connection between the smuggling scheme and the sabotage of Nancy's plane!

For a quick solution, turn to page 69.
To investigate further, turn to page 75.

Frank waited while Joe and Nancy ducked into the hangar. A moment later, a woman appeared out of the shadows and followed the young detectives. Frank walked behind her at a safe distance.

"Are you the Hardys?" the woman called to Joe and Nancy with a faint accent.

The two faced the stranger. She was small, with delicate features and sensitive eyes. And she was clearly frightened.

"I'm Joe Hardy," Joe said, extending his hand. "And this is my friend, Nancy Drew."

The woman looked perplexed. "Oh!" she said. "I thought there were two Hardy brothers."

Frank stepped from the shadows and introduced himself. "There are," he said. "I'm Frank. What can we do for you?"

The woman sighed. "It is all so confusing," she said. "I am Dolores Salazar. Ernesto Salazar is my brother. His life is in danger. You must help me save him."

Turn to page 61.

The Hardys greeted their friend and hugged her in relief.

"Next time," Frank teased her, "could you try for a less dramatic appearance?"

Nancy grinned. "I didn't exactly plan this, you know."

Later, when they were all seated around the kitchen table in the Hardy home, the boys' Aunt Gertrude put a plate of fresh buttermilk biscuits in front of them. She clucked her tongue in distress. "It seems as if you're faced with another mystery," she said. "And I don't like it. Here Nancy comes to help investigate a smuggling case, and almost doesn't make it because someone sabotaged her plane! I don't like it one bit!"

"I think there's a connection between the case and my near accident," Nancy spoke up. "Perhaps someone wants the investigation stopped!"

"It could be somebody in Salazar's importing company," Frank added. "We'll drive to New York as soon as we're finished eating and start checking the place out."

Half an hour later, the young detectives were on their way with Frank behind the wheel. Soon after they had left Bayport, a large black car pulled alongside their yellow sports sedan.

"Look out, Frank!" Nancy screamed.

Turn to page 65.

Nancy inched toward a fire ax hanging on the wall as Sergio disappeared into the office. The truck was beginning to move. Nancy grabbed the ax. When the truck was heading out of the warehouse, she swung it hard against the thin cable suspending the door overhead. The cable was severed with a single blow, dropping the door like a giant knife onto the truck and knocking the driver unconscious.

There was no time for Nancy to reach the container holding the prisoners. The fat man bounded out of the office in a rage. "Who are you?—Nancy Drew! I should have known."

Nancy darted behind a tall pile of stacked wooden boxes, and pushed them. The crates toppled to the floor, burying the man in splintered wood and thousands of tiny clay pots made in Mexico. "Help!" Sergio shouted, but he couldn't move.

Nancy jumped onto the truck and set the trapped young men free. "I've got a hunch those old packing crates hold the solution to this scheme," she told them.

Turn to page 97.

Joe drove to Manhattan, where Salazar's importing company was located.

Two hours later, the three were standing across the street from a combination warehouse and office. Nancy glanced at the weathered sign above the door. "I can tell you one thing," she said. "The s.i.c. on the coin does not stand for Salazar Importing Company." She pointed to the sign: SALAZAR IMPORTS.

"Then s.i.c. must be a person," Joe said.

Nancy nodded. "And my guess is that person is in there right now! You investigate the alley. I'm going into the office."

"Be careful," Frank said as he and Joe slipped out of sight down the narrow alley next to the warehouse.

To stay with the boys, turn to page 19.
To follow Nancy, turn to page 71.

The criminals drove to Bayport Harbor, then stopped in front of a small building.

"That's our boathouse!" Joe exclaimed.

"That's right," Sergio said. Then he turned to Nancy. "I didn't think you'd survive your flight," he said. "But then I didn't count on your intrepid friends. I should have known they would never let you down. This time will be different, though, because you're all going to be lost at sea *together!*"

The two men herded their prisoners into the *Sleuth*. "The Coast Guard thinks you Hardys are still out on the bay looking for Miss Drew's plane," Sergio went on. "Well, they're going to find you, all unfortunate victims of a double tragedy—a plane crash and boating accident!"

Turn to page 93.

Several minutes later, the Hardys came into the hangar.

"Nancy's gone!" Joe exclaimed.

Frank nodded in dismay. "My guess is that whoever wrote that note has captured her," he said and glanced around the empty building. "But where have they gone?"

"Look," Joe said, pointing to the oil spot on the floor. "Footprints."

Two perfect sets of oily footprints started at the puddle and led outside. The detectives went after them. "If I know Nancy, she did that on purpose," Frank said. "She would try to leave a clue for us."

The Hardy brothers followed the marks, which pointed toward the parking lot. "They're wearing out," Joe said. "Wait right here. I'll be back in a minute."

When he returned, he had a sprinkling can filled with water in his hand. Frank smiled at his brother's ingenuity as Joe poured several drops on the last clear set of footprints. A colorful pattern of oil rose to the top of the puddle he made. Carefully, Joe let out more water all around him, bringing to light the hidden footsteps until they finally stopped.

"This is where Nancy and her abductor got into a car," he deduced.

Turn to the next page.

Frank spotted a man crossing the parking lot, and he ran up to him. "Excuse me, sir, did you happen to see a girl get into a car over there?" he asked, pointing to where Joe stood.

The man shook his head. "Nope. Sorry," he said. "Did see a pretty young thing with reddish hair get in a truck, though. Her and a big guy. Just five minutes ago."

"Thanks!" Frank ran after Joe, who was already heading for their yellow sports sedan.

"I heard," Joe said as he started the engine. Then he drove to the toll booth at the parking lot exit and spoke to the attendant.

"Yeah, a truck just came by here," the toll taker said. "Turned left as soon as it went out the gate. Up Parker Hill Road."

The Hardys zoomed up Parker Hill Road. "This leads to the abandoned granite quarry," Frank commented with a worried look. The quarry was a place where people took things they wanted to have disappear forever.

Turn to page 81.

Later that day the three friends were about to land at the airport in Mexico City. "It's a tragedy what pollution has done to this beautiful city," Nancy commented.

Frank and Joe nodded sadly. The Valley of Mexico, a vast plain 8,000 feet above sea level, had been turned into a cauldron of industrial smog.

The investigators reviewed the case as they rode in a creeping cab through jammed traffic up the Avenida Reforma.

"Salazar suspects someone is smuggling stolen artifacts in crates that are shipped from here to his New York City warehouse," Frank said. "His observations are based on one small piece of broken pottery he found in a recent shipment of pots."

"Isn't that to be expected?" Nancy asked as she admired the beautiful flowers and palm trees along Mexico City's loveliest avenue.

Frank shook his head. "Not when the broken piece is over nine hundred years old," he said.

Turn to page 85.

"Tell us all you know," Joe said gently.

"Ernesto and I own the Salazar Importing Company," Dolores went on. "A month ago an art dealer named Guzman engaged us to ship goods from Mexico to his gallery in New York City. My brother became suspicious when he opened one of the shipments and found items which were not on the shipping list."

"That's why he suspects Guzman of smuggling art goods?" Joe asked.

"Yes," Dolores replied. "But when Ernesto went to Guzman about it, the man threatened to tell the authorities that it was my *brother* who was smuggling."

"And so Ernesto hired our dad to investigate," Frank concluded.

The woman nodded. "Yes, but Guzman does not know your father is a detective. He is having my brother and your father followed every minute they are in Mexico. If he finds out, he will have them killed."

"We have to warn Mr. Hardy and Ernesto Salazar," Nancy declared.

Turn to page 68.

Nancy and Frank arrived in the hangar in time to hear Salazar's story of blackmail. "We have a cousin in Mexico," Ernesto told them. "Each month he sends a small package inside our regular shipment of imported goods to our warehouse in New York City. He forbids us to open it. A man we do not know comes to pick it up the day it arrives."

"Why don't you go to the police?" Frank inquired.

"If we do, my cousin says he will inform the Mexican authorities we are smugglers and our business will be ruined," replied Salazar.

"Blackmail," Nancy stated correctly.

"When is the next shipment due?" Joe asked.

"It is being loaded on my truck right now," Salazar replied. "We had it rerouted to Bayport because there is a freight workers' strike expected at all airports in New York. When I saw you, I put the note on your car to give you a message from your father in secret, because the man who picks up the smuggled goods has become suspicious and may be watching."

"You have a message from our father?" Frank asked. "What is it?"

"Stop your investigation," Salazar said.

"Dad wants us to stop?" Joe exclaimed in disbelief.

"Yes," Salazar said sharply. "Now! Otherwise you will endanger his investigation!"

Turn to the next page.

"That doesn't sound like Dad at all," Frank said as the nervous man in the green shirt drove off in his truck. "I think we should follow Salazar to New York City."

Nancy and Joe quickly agreed, and the sleuths secretly tailed the truck in their yellow sports sedan for the two-hour journey to Manhattan.

"Once we learn who's receiving the smuggled goods we'll radio Dad," Joe said. "He can inform the Mexican authorities while we go to the New York police."

"If nothing happens in the meantime," Frank suggested cautiously as the truck disappeared into a rundown warehouse in lower Manhattan. He parked the yellow sedan in a concealed spot and the three hid behind another building.

Sometime later, a man in a red shirt, his face obscured by shadows, emerged from the warehouse carrying a small package under his arm. He glanced nervously over his shoulder as he hurried to a waiting car and quickly drove off.

"You follow him," Frank said to Joe and Nancy. "I'll go inside and check on Salazar."

To follow the man with Joe and Nancy,
   turn to page 73.
To check on Salazar with Frank, turn to page 76.

For the second time that day, the three investigators were at Bayport Airport. As they hurried to the reservation counter, Joe seemed troubled.

"Come on," Frank called. "We've just enough time to get tickets. What's bothering you?"

"I'm not sure," Joe replied as they waited their turn. "Dad's voice sounded, well, *odd,* didn't you think?"

Frank nodded. "I noticed the same thing, but I suppose it's because of the international telephone connection. After all, he was calling all the way from Mexico City."

"*Was* he?" Joe seemed unconvinced.

"What do you mean?" Nancy asked, her curiosity piqued.

Just then the ticket agent approached. "Ah, Miss Drew and the Hardy brothers. I've been expecting you. Here are your tickets. Mr. Hardy just called from Mexico City. He said he spoke with you earlier."

Frank, Joe, and Nancy hid their surprise. They knew they had not spoken with Mr. Hardy!

Turn to page 121.

Frank clutched the wheel. The black car was trying to force them off the road!

"Hang on!" he shouted and slammed on the brakes. The other car shot past them. Just when its driver started to slow down, Frank accelerated again. The Hardys passed the black car and Frank cut in front of it.

The other driver, confused by the boy's maneuver, had stepped on the gas again and now had to swerve to avoid a collision. He went into a skid, wobbled for a moment, then slid off the edge of the road into a ditch. There he turned over.

Frank stopped and the young people jumped out of their sedan. A moment later, their antagonist tumbled out the door of his car. Joe and Nancy leaped on him before he had a chance to get up. Meanwhile, Frank examined the black car for other occupants. There were none.

"Who are you working for?" Joe demanded of the dazed driver.

"I don't know what you're talking about," he replied.

Turn to the next page.

Frank was just coming around from the back of the overturned car, where he had examined the trunk, which had popped open in the accident.

"Maybe this will help you remember," he said.

Turn to the next page.

He held a large aerosol can in his hand. The label read: PLASTIC INSULATING FOAM.

"It's the same stuff that was used to fill my plane's tanks!" Nancy exclaimed and gave the man an angry look.

He cringed. "Salazar's bookkeeper made me do it," he said. "He's smuggling artifacts from Mexico through the company. I went to River Heights to sabotage the plane because he told me to do it. He said Fenton Hardy would uncover the smuggling plot unless something happened to distract him."

"So the bookkeeper figured if Nancy didn't make it to Bayport, we'd drop the investigation, is that it?" Joe asked angrily.

The man nodded. It was clear that he and his accomplice had no idea how determined Nancy Drew and the Hardys were, and that they would stick to a case no matter what happened.

The young detectives took the man to the nearest police station. The local chief alerted the New York authorities, who arrested the bookkeeper promptly. A few days later, Mr. Salazar, the Hardys, and Nancy had dinner together.

"You did a wonderful job!" the importer praised the young people.

Frank grinned. "Dad once taught us a lesson in evasive tactics used to protect people from kidnapping attempts," he replied. "It sure came in handy for catching the crook in the black car!"

END

Frank quickly called Sam Radley, Mr. Hardy's trusted operative, from a nearby phone booth. "Sam, would you get in touch with Dad and Ernesto Salazar in Mexico City?" he asked. "Tell them they're being shadowed by a guy working for a New York art dealer named Guzman. Guzman's on to them."

"Don't worry about your dad," Sam said. "He knows how to take care of himself. But I'll call him right away."

When Frank had rejoined the others, he said, "We can work out the problem on this end. Let's go to New York and check out Guzman's art gallery."

"Good idea," Dolores Salazar said, and the group got into the Hardys' car. On the way to New York, Nancy was staring at Dolores's handbag. This seemed to make the woman nervous. "Is something wrong?" she asked.

Nancy shook her head. "Oh, no. I was just admiring your purse. It's beautiful."

Later the four sat in an ice-cream parlor across the street from the gallery. "We can't take the chance of having Guzman see you with us," Nancy said to Dolores. "Why don't you go to your office and wait for our call?"

"Yes, of course," the woman said and quickly left.

Just then a man walked out of the gallery with a package under his arm. He turned and locked the door behind him.

"That must be Guzman!" Frank said.

Turn to page 122.

A large black car pulled into the alley behind Salazar's warehouse. The investigators watched it from their hiding place. The driver got out and entered the building.

Frank peered through a dust-covered window. "He's making a phone call," he said. "But I can't hear what he's saying."

As Joe and Chet joined Frank at the window, Nancy scurried around to the area where the trash bin had been. She found what she was looking for and returned to the others. In her hand was a cardboard cylinder, the kind paper towels are wrapped around. She placed one end against the window and put her ear to the other. "Sshh," she said. "I can hear him now."

She relayed what the man was saying. "He's calling Mexico City, telling someone my plane crashed but he doesn't know where I am. Now he's ordering the other person to stop the smuggling operation because he knows your dad is investigating."

The three conferred quickly. "If they stop, Dad won't be able to find any evidence," Frank pointed out.

"We have to get the smugglers to think Dad is off the case," Joe concluded.

Turn to the next page.

The sleuths drove back to the Hardy house in Bayport. They went directly to the short-wave radio, and Joe placed a call to his father. "They're on to your investigation, Dad," the boy reported. "They sabotaged Nancy's plane. She's okay, but they don't know that."

Fenton Hardy thought fast. "Obviously they want us to drop the case," he said. "Well, we'll give them what they want. Here's what I want you to do . . ."

For the next few minutes, the famous detective spelled out his plan to trap the smugglers.

Turn to page 51.

Nancy slipped into the office. It was quiet and appeared to be empty. Suddenly a rough voice broke the silence. "What do you want?"

A gruff-looking man stared at Nancy from a desk behind a partition. "Oh, I'm sorry," Nancy said. "I'm at the wrong address." She turned quickly and headed for the door. But just as she was about to leave, a dark-haired woman with sad eyes entered, carrying a tray of coffee and sandwiches.

"What took you so long with those sandwiches, Sylvia?" the man demanded. "You make them yourself?"

The woman glanced briefly into Nancy's eyes. Nancy noticed a dark, frightened look, the look of someone very nervous or very scared.

She hurried out the door and went back to the yellow sports sedan to wait for Frank and Joe. Then she gasped. Traced in the dust on the side of the car was the word HELP. And beneath it were the initials S.I.C.

Turn to the next page.

A few minutes later, Frank and Joe returned. They looked at the initials on the car in surprise.

"These were not there when we left the airport," Frank declared. "Someone must have written them since we arrived here."

Nancy grinned. "I know who did it and I can tell you her name if you cross my palm with silver!"

"Huh?" Frank was puzzled.

Joe gave Nancy the Mexican coin.

"Not that kind of silver," she said. "The good old American kind. Dimes."

Frank and Joe huddled around Nancy as they listened to her make a phone call with their coins. "May I speak with Sylvia . . . er, oh dear, I've forgotten her last name," Nancy said when someone on the other end answered the call. "Oh, yes, that's it. Sylvia Indo-Cruz." She winked at the boys. Then she spoke into the phone again, "Sylvia. We got your message. Meet us at the diner at Twenty-third Street and Tenth Avenue on your lunch break." Then she hung up.

Turn to page 80.

The man with the package drove out of Manhattan and finally turned onto a narrow country lane far from the city. He pulled into the circular drive of an elegant country estate. Joe parked the yellow sports sedan where it couldn't be seen, and the two investigators sneaked around to the side of the house and peered in a window.

"It looks like a museum!" Nancy gasped.

Hundreds of precious artifacts from all over the world lined the room. The man sat at a large ornate desk and unwrapped the package. He took out a magnificent figure of an Aztec warrior and set it on the desk. It was carved out of natural crystal rock.

"It's the most beautiful thing I've ever seen!" Nancy exclaimed.

Before Joe could respond, a pair of gloved hands reached around from behind him and Nancy and banged their heads together stunning them for several minutes.

When the two investigators came to, they were tied together, back to back, in what they assumed to be the cellar of the huge mansion. A musty, cold draft and the steady drip, drip, drip of water told them they were deep under the building.

Turn to the next page.

"Whoever knocked us out and tied these knots did an excellent job," Joe grumbled. He flexed his wrists but the bonds were too tight to slip off.

Nancy was thinking. "Can you stand up, Joe?" she asked.

Joe moved. "Yes," he said. "My legs are free."

"Mine, too," Nancy said. "Do you hear that water?"

"Yes," Joe answered, wondering what Nancy was getting at.

"If we hop over to the water and let it drip on these ropes, maybe we can stretch them enough to get free," Nancy said.

The two detectives hobbled to the wall where a trickle of water dripped to the cellar floor. They turned so the water fell on the ropes and kept flexing their wrists even though it hurt. Finally, after long, agonizing work, the ropes loosened.

"I'm out!" Joe exclaimed.

"So am I," Nancy said.

"Now, let's see where our host is," Joe said.

The young detectives searched for an exit from the cellar, but found none. "We'll have to go this way," Joe whispered, and pointed to a long staircase. "I hope no one's guarding the door on top."

Silently the two climbed up to the main floor of the mansion and opened the door at the end of the staircase. They found themselves in a large entrance hall. It was empty.

Turn to page 87.

The young detectives searched around the warehouse, but found no other clues. They returned to Bayport and, even though it was already past midnight, they studied the strange piece of foam that Nancy had found in the trash bin.

"This was used to make an impression of something," the girl said as she held the white plastic beneath a strong light.

"Like a mold?" Joe asked.

"Precisely," she replied. She mixed a small pot of fast-drying clay, which she poured into the impression in the plastic material. When it was dry, she pried away the foam.

"Wow!" Joe exclaimed as he examined the casting Nancy had made. It was a piece of a small statue, the head of an Aztec idol called the Feathered Serpent. He recognized it from a picture he had seen recently.

"That's the smuggling scheme," Frank declared. "They're not smuggling real artifacts—just the molds!"

Turn to page 82.

Frank ducked into the dark warehouse. The truck they had followed was parked in the middle of the big building. Although he heard no voices and saw no movement, Frank sensed there was someone nearby. He lifted the canvas flap closing the rear of the vehicle. Inside were a number of heavy wooden boxes. And sticking out from between two of the crates was a pair of men's feet!

Frank leaped onto the truck and threw open the canvas. He directed his flashlight at the man on the floor, who groaned. The young detective stared in disbelief.

To learn why Frank was so shocked, turn to page 78.
For a strange twist, turn to page 79.

Nancy pulled the two boys into the lobby, planning to explain. But before they could speak to one another, the man with the package suddenly stepped out from behind a potted palm and aimed a gun at them. The doorman looked the other way.

"You are too clever for your own good!" the art dealer hissed. "How did you know Dolores is my wife and not Ernesto Salazar's sister?"

Nancy shrugged. "I saw the tiny monogram on her handbag—D.G. I wasn't quite sure, but then I noticed the names on the mailboxes. Among the tenants are Diego and Dolores Guzman."

"Then the whole thing was a trick to trap us!" Joe exploded.

"And to get dad to stop his investigaton!" Frank added.

Guzman grinned. "We need only a few days to sell the smuggled items that were stolen from the National Museum in Mexico City. With your father warned and you in our custody, we won't have any trouble."

He led his prisoners to the elevator, and a moment later the door slammed shut.

Guzman pushed the button for the tenth floor. "You see," he said with an evil grin, "we planned it perfectly."

"Not quite," Frank said. Then he turned to his friends. "Hit the deck!" he shouted suddenly.

Turn to page 88.

"Dad!" Frank exclaimed.

Fenton Hardy lay on the truck bed. He had a lump the size of a ripe olive over his right eye. "What happened?" the boy asked and cradled his father's head in his arms.

"Ernesto Salazar is the smuggler," Fenton Hardy said as he regained his senses.

"But where's his brother Enrico?" Frank asked.

The famous private detective recovered quickly. "There is no Enrico," he said. "Only Ernesto. He made up a brother to throw off my investigation."

"But *he* was the one who hired you to investigate the smuggling scheme," Frank said.

"That's what he thought, Frank," Mr. Hardy said. "It was U.S. customs agents who first brought me into the case. They knew Salazar was smuggling artifacts from Mexico, but they had no proof. Salazar suspected something so he hired me hoping I'd tell him about the customs investigation and its results."

"Why was he going to Mexico with you?" Frank asked.

"He said he would accompany me to check out that end of the case," Fenton Hardy said, "but he never really intended to leave. At five o'clock this morning, as we were boarding our plane in New York, he made up an excuse and told me to go on ahead, saying he would take a later flight."

Turn to page 111.

The man lying on the truck bed was dressed in the same green shirt that Ernesto Salazar had been wearing at the airport, but his face looked different! He stared groggily at Frank, whom he recognized immediately. "Frank Hardy," he whispered, rubbing a lump on his head.

"Yes," Frank replied. "But who are you?"

"I am Ernesto Salazar," the man said, sitting up. "The man who just ran from here in my clothes was my brother, Enrico. He's the smuggler."

In Salazar's office, the real Ernesto explained his brother's smuggling scheme and showed Frank the evidence that Fenton Hardy had uncovered in Mexico. "I became suspicious of my brother so I hired your father, who found these documents," he said. "They are proof enough to convict Enrico. I returned to confront him while your father stayed in Mexico to help catch Enrico's accomplices there. I told Enrico to give himself up . . . ."

"But he refused," Frank added with understanding. "And when he saw us at the airport, he suspected we were investigating the case, too, so he pretended to be you to throw us off his trail long enough to get away."

Turn to page 86.

Sylvia Indo-Cruz was very nervous when she arrived at the diner and joined the three investigators in a booth. "Somebody is blackmailing my brother in Mexico to smuggle stolen artifacts in Mr. Salazar's crates," she said.

"Can you let us into the warehouse tonight?" Joe asked. "We've got to find out what's being smuggled."

"I think so," Sylvia agreed hesitantly.

Late that night she met the young detectives at the warehouse. "You must hurry," she said. "I heard my boss say someone is coming at ten for a shipment." Then she left.

Frank stroked his chin. "With luck we may learn what's being smuggled and catch the smugglers, too."

Inside, the detectives searched for clues. Before they found any, Nancy and the Hardys heard a noise and hid just before the lights went on. An elegantly dressed man entered. He opened a large crate marked HECHO EN MEXICO and removed a clay pot. He looked at its bottom, shook his head, and proceeded to examine each pot in the crate until he found the one he wanted.

Then he repacked all the pots except the one he had come for, and left the building.

To follow the man, turn to page 83.

The boys parked in back of a knoll and hid behind a rock where they could watch the quarry below without being seen. "There she is!" Joe exclaimed in a low tone.

A man held Nancy at the edge of the water-filled quarry; it was clear he was going to throw her in. She could not survive in the water very long since her hands were tied. She'd be gone by the time the boys reached her.

"We have to scare him off before he pushes her," Frank declared. "But there are only the two of us!"

"He doesn't know that," Joe pointed out. He cupped his hands to his mouth and began to wail like a siren, filling the air with the shrill sound of a police car. It reverberated in the quarry where the man froze in indecision.

"You are surrounded," Frank shouted at the top of his voice. "Let the girl go and put your hands up."

Joe continued to wail like a siren. It was their only chance to save Nancy!

The man panicked. He let Nancy go and ran to his truck. A moment later, he disappeared down the road in a cloud of dust. The boys rushed to Nancy, who was trying to loosen the bonds that held her.

"I think I have a clue as to who that scared rabbit is," she reported matter-of-factly, even though she was still shaking with fright.

Turn to page 90.

While Frank and Chet studied the intricate clay head Nancy had cast in the broken foam mold, Joe tuned the short-wave radio in the crime lab. In minutes, the voice of Fenton Hardy crackled over the air from Mexico.

"My investigation shows nothing is being smuggled out of here through Salazar's company," Mr. Hardy reported with a note of discouragement in his voice.

"That's just it, Dad," Joe said. "They're smuggling *nothing*." He explained how hollow molds were made from precious artifacts and used as "packing material" in legitimate shipments through Salazar's company.

"Aha!" Fenton Hardy exclaimed. "Then the crooks make copies and sell them as the real thing. That explains why nothing is missing from any of the museums down here." He paused. "But *who* is doing it?"

"I think I have a way to find out," Nancy said.

Turn to page 84.

The three detectives followed and saw him hail a taxi outside. They quickly got into their car and followed the cab.

"I'm not quite sure," Joe said, "but I have a feeling that the man we're chasing is R. Burton Totten."

"The art collector?" Nancy asked in surprise.

"Yes. I recognized him from a TV interview."

The cab stopped in front of a well-known Fifth Avenue art gallery and the man got out.

"You were right, Joe!" Frank said. "It's Totten. This is his gallery."

"What'll we do now?" Nancy asked. "Follow him inside or come back in the morning?"

If you think the detectives should come back in the morning, turn to page 23.

To continue the investigation right now, turn to page 89.

The next morning, Nancy dialed Salazar's office. "Salazar Importing," a man answered.

"This is People's Airlines," Nancy said in a disguised voice. "We've located the luggage you lost on your recent trip to River Heights."

"I didn't go to River Heights," the man said. "That was Drake. I'll get him."

Frank and Joe, who were standing close to Nancy and had heard the conversation, nodded enthusiastically. Nancy's deduction was correct. Someone at Salazar's company had come to her hometown and sabotaged her plane.

The man returned to the phone. "He didn't lose any luggage," he said. "Hey! Who is this?"

Nancy hung up. "Now we know definitely that someone at Salazar Importing is involved in the smuggling scheme. All we have to do is smoke him out."

"I have a plan," Joe said. "Let's go back to New York."

When the young detectives arrived in the city, Joe dialed Salazar's office again from a phone booth.

Turn to page 105.

The cab stopped in front of a giant traffic island in the center of the broad avenue. Rising above it was a white stone obelisk topped by the magnificent gold statue of a winged angel.

"The Angel," Nancy said. "It's one of the most beautiful pieces of sculpture of its kind I know."

Frank and Joe were searching the traffic island for their father. Cars and buses swarmed around like a school of steel sharks, but there was no sign of Fenton Hardy.

Just then a small blue Volkswagen taxi pulled up in front of the trio. Its driver waved. "Hardy?" he asked.

The young investigators nodded. The man signaled for them to get in his cab.

Soon the taxi was whizzing up a narrow road in the country. The city was far behind in the valley. "This is Contadero," the driver said in Spanish. "It means the 'counting place.' It is where they counted the gold in the days of the conquistadores." He smiled at his passengers through the rearview mirror. "Some say there is buried treasure here."

He stopped in front of a small hotel. Fenton Hardy was waiting for them in the lobby.

Turn to page 92.

"Yes," Ernesto responded, amazed at Frank's grasp of the complex case. "I pleaded with him a few moments ago to give himself up, but he knocked me out. And now he's gone."

Frank smiled wryly. "Gone but not forgotten," he replied as he picked up the phone and dialed a special number. "My brother Joe and Nancy Drew are following your brother. They have a telephone in the car and can tell us where he's headed."

Frank spoke briefly with Joe, then hung up the phone. "Enrico is at an abandoned building on a pier at the Hudson River where he has hidden his smuggled merchandise. I'll call the police, and then we'll go there, too, because Joe and Nancy may need our help."

Turn to page 96.

Nancy pointed across the hall. Muffled voices came from one of the rooms. "That's where they are," she whispered. The two sleuths silently crept up to the door and hid behind a heavy, carved chest that stood next to it. Now they could hear the voices inside clearly.

"What'll we do with them snoopy kids?" a man asked gruffly.

"Get rid of them," another replied.

A moment later, the door opened and a thick-chested man stepped out. He headed for the cellar.

"Let's lock him in once he's down there," Joe whispered.

Nancy nodded with a smile. Her head still hurt from the attack by the window. When the man had disappeared down the stairs, she crept from behind the chest and walked to the open stairway. "Are you looking for us?" she asked the big man.

He whirled around. "How'd you get loose?" he demanded, then charged up the steps like a mad bull.

But Nancy closed the door and bolted it before he reached the top.

Joe walked toward her and took her arm. "Come on," he urged.

Turn to page 101.

Nancy and Joe quickly dropped to the floor at the same moment. Frank punched the emergency stop button and turned out the lights. The elevator jammed to a sudden halt. It was pitch black inside.

Frank knew that Guzman was still standing in the same spot. He clenched his fist and threw a solid punch through the darkness. It landed soundly on Guzman's jaw, knocking him cold.

When the New York City police took the Guzmans away half an hour later, Frank, Joe, and Nancy returned to the ice-cream parlor across the street from the gallery.

"That was a great bit of detective work, Nancy," Frank said proudly. "It's sure proof that sometimes three heads are better than two when it comes to solving a mystery."

"Or when it's time to dig into a Super Treat Sundae," Nancy said as she put her spoon into a mammoth tub of ice cream containing the ten flavors the three had ordered to celebrate!

END

Totten unlocked the front door of the art gallery and entered. The three investigators hurried to the side of the building where they wouldn't be seen.

"The front part of the place is only one story," Joe said. "If we can get onto the roof, maybe there's a skylight."

One by one, they climbed up a drainpipe, then searched the roof. As Joe suspected, a skylight, illuminated from a lamp in the room below, permitted them to see in. Totten sat at his desk with the mysterious clay pot before him.

"It doesn't look like anything I'd bother to smuggle," Nancy whispered. "Kind of plain, don't you think?"

Suddenly Totten smashed the pot with a small hammer. The red clay pieces fell away to reveal a magnificent, shiny feather, as delicate as a real one, but crafted in exquisite gold!

"It *is* a smuggling operation," Frank exclaimed in a low tone.

"Yes," Joe said. "Artifacts are brought out of Mexico through Salazar's company in ordinary clay pots."

"Very clear, my young meddlers," a man suddenly hissed behind them.

The investigators were stunned. A shiny blue gun pointed at them from the shadows.

Turn to page 91.

"Who?" Frank asked.

"Let's get into the car and I'll tell you."

As Joe drove the yellow sedan out of the quarry, Nancy explained. "The three strands of this rope are green, white, and red," she said, displaying the cord that had bound her. "Those are the colors of the Mexican flag. My guess is this is decorative rope—"

"Used by someone promoting goods from Mexico," Frank interrupted. "Like, perhaps, the Salazar Importing Company?"

Nancy nodded. "I think a visit to their place is in order. But this time, let's call the police to back us up."

Later that day, the three detectives were walking around the New York City warehouse of the Salazar Importing Company. Parked in front was the truck from the quarry. "The man is in there," Nancy said, cautiously peering into an open window. "It looks like he's about to leave."

Joe winked at the others. "I think I know how to stop him," he said.

Turn to page 98.

They had to follow their captor from the roof.

A few minutes later, the three detectives were in Totten's office. The man with the gun kept a steady eye on them. "You were right, Mr. Totten," he said. "There *was* somebody following you."

"The famous Hardys and Miss Nancy Drew," R. Burton Totten said. "It's too bad, because now that they've discovered my smuggling operation, I'll have to get rid of them."

He fondled the magnificent gold feather. "My plan will be complete in one more move," he said. He lifted a cloth covering a tall object on his desk. Beneath it was a fantastic golden serpent, covered with finely crafted gold feathers. He set the latest arrival in its place. "You see, only one more feather to go and I will own the famous Feathered Serpent."

"But we have the last feather!" Frank said.

Totten stared blankly at the three investigators. "That's impossible. It's still in Mexico."

Frank shook his head. "The sister of the man you were blackmailing to smuggle the artifact showed us the pot with the last feather," he declared. "It's already in the warehouse."

Nancy and Joe were surprised at Frank's announcement, but did not show it. Obviously he had a plan.

"We'll see soon enough!" Totten rasped. "And if you're lying, you'll pay the price." He nodded to his guard. "Get the car. We'll drive to the warehouse."

Turn to page 94.

After dinner, the handsome detective explained what he'd uncovered in his investigation as the young friends sipped manzanilla tea.

"Mr. Salazar had to go back to New York, so I called you to help me. So far, there's no evidence that artifacts are being smuggled. In fact, nothing has been reported stolen or missing from the museums." He held up a very old piece of broken pottery. "The only evidence we have is this. It's what made Salazar suspicious."

Frank, Nancy, and Joe examined the old potsherd. They compared it with an archeologist's sketch of what the pot would have looked like whole. It resembled an ordinary jug.

"This is the kind of container people stored things in, isn't it?" Frank asked.

Fenton Hardy nodded. "My investigation traced it to this area. The answer lies somewhere right here in the village of Contadero."

Joe frowned. "But what's the question?" he asked.

"The kind of artifacts that are being smuggled," Mr. Hardy said, somewhat surprised.

"Maybe artifacts aren't being smuggled," Joe said. "Remember what the cab driver said about gold being hidden around here?"

Frank and Nancy nodded.

Turn to page 100.

As his henchman steered the *Sleuth* through the waves, Sergio guarded his prisoners. "I knew we'd have trouble with our smuggling scheme if the famous Fenton Hardy was investigating in Mexico and you meddlers were poking your noses in here," he said. "I was sure that if Miss Drew were missing at sea, Mr. Hardy would return to check out her 'accident' and drop the smuggling case. Well, you can be sure he'll stop working on it now when he hears that Miss Drew *and* his sons are missing."

"Hey, what about me?" Chet asked. He had been able to slip out of the ropes that tied his hands, but kept his wrists together so no one would notice.

"Next time you'll learn to mind your own business," the man said. "Except, there won't be a next time."

He turned to his henchman. "Stop the boat," he ordered.

The *Sleuth* drifted to a standstill on the bobbing waves.

"Now, if you don't mind, I'd like you to step over the side," Sergio said with a sneer.

Chet shot a quick glance at the others. Then he twisted his face in fear. "I can't swim," he screamed.

"That's the idea," the man said. "Now jump!"

Turn to page 112.

On the way to Salazar Imports, the man with the gun didn't take his eyes off the young detectives. Still, Frank managed to tap a message in code to his companions: "Joe and I get gun . . . Nancy, get Totten on signal."

Once all five were in the gloomy warehouse, Totten grabbed Frank by the arm. "Which pot has the feather?" he asked anxiously.

"It's up there," the boy replied, pointing to a crate stacked high overhead. "I'll get it."

He climbed the stack, picked up a heavy pot from the crate, and held it above his head. "Here," he said. Then, to Joe and Nancy, he shouted, "Now!"

He flung the pot at the man with the gun who staggered and fell. Joe grabbed the gun. Nancy immediately threw a karate chop at Totten, who flopped to the floor like a dead fish. In minutes the smugglers were prisoners and the young detectives their captors.

"Dad'll be pleased to hear we've cracked the smuggling scheme," Joe said. "And he'll be able to tell Sylvia's brother that he's free from blackmail."

Sylvia was overjoyed when she heard from the sleuths the next day. "Please keep the coin," she said. "It is very valuable and was in my family for a long time. But now I want you to have it for helping us. I'm sure my brother feels that way, too."

END

Soon Frank and Ernesto Salazar were at the abandoned pier where a ramshackle building sagged dangerously on rotting pilings over the black water of the mighty Hudson River. Sudden flashes of light from among a clutter of junk on the pier caught Frank's attention. He grabbed Ernesto by the arm as the two were about to enter the old building.

"Your brother knows we're here," Frank whispered. He gestured toward the pile of junk. "Joe and Nancy are hiding behind there. Joe just flashed a message to me in code telling me that Enrico spotted us."

As he spoke, another ominous warning in code came from Joe and Nancy's hiding place.

To go to Joe and Nancy, turn to page 103.
To stay with Frank and Ernesto, turn to page 116.
For a surprise ending, turn to page 118.

Nancy compared the crate the boys had been put in with several others from the pile that the fat man wanted delivered.

"Look!" she cried. "The boards on this box are less than a half-inch thick. But these special ones over here are almost an inch thick!"

As the three young men watched, she pulled out her Swiss army knife and pried at a box from the suspicious stack, trying to split one of its boards lengthwise. Sure enough, part of it broke off to reveal a hollow section between the two halves. It was filled with tiny electronic components.

"Computer chips!" Joe exclaimed.

"So that's it," Frank said to Ricardo Salazar. "Your uncle wasn't smuggling artifacts or treasure. He was smuggling computer chips."

"Ooooohhh," the fat man moaned from beneath the pile of tumbled crates.

Nancy and the Hardys smiled. "He'll have plenty of time in jail to recover," the girl said. "I'll call the police."

Ricardo shook the investigators' hands as two detectives took the smugglers away. "For my father and me, I wish to thank you," he said.

"And we want to thank you for the clue that helped us solve the case," Frank returned.

END

He cupped his hands and blew another wailing siren. The man froze in his tracks.

"The cops have followed me here," he cried out dejectedly. "It's no use trying to get away. They'll follow me wherever I go."

When the police arrived, a moment later, the three young detectives told them what they had overheard. Two officers went into the office and questioned the criminal, who admitted everything. He was Salazar's partner, and was smuggling goods from Mexico. When he had learned that the Hardys and Nancy Drew were on his track, he decided to foil the investigation by getting rid of one of them, thinking the others would give up and look for the kidnapped member of their group. That would give him time to escape.

"A couple of simple clues foiled *him*," Joe said. "An oily footprint and a serpent."

Nancy and Frank scratched their heads. "What serpent?" they asked.

Joe coiled the green, white, and red rope beneath a Mexican flag in Salazar's office. On the flag was the symbol of Mexico, an eagle with a serpent in its talons. "This one," he said, flicking the rope like a snake. "And we were the eagles."

END

Frank and Joe watched from behind a concrete bridge abutment as the burly man led Nancy to the water's edge. "We'd better let her know we're here," Frank said. He blew a shrill bird call that contained four letters in Morse code, "U . . . R . . . O . . . K".

That's what they think, Nancy thought. But her friends' message had given her hope.

"Any last words?" Lorraine asked Nancy.

"Yes," Nancy said. "Remember, crime never pays."

The woman laughed, but stopped when she saw the Hardys and five uniformed officers of the New York City Police Department descend on the scene, completely surprising the hoodlums.

Later, after Lorraine and her accomplices had confessed to the smuggling operation, the three sleuths enjoyed Aunt Gertrude's lunch which was served in the sun behind the stately Hardy house on Elm Street. "Lorraine knew that with Dad on her trail in Mexico it would all be over soon," Frank said. "She planned to pull one last job, but then she heard we were investigating here. She had to stop us . . . ."

"And that's where she made her mistake. Nothing can stop the forces of law," Aunt gertrude declared. The young people smiled. Even though Aunt Gertrude often complained about their detective work, she was very, very proud of them.

END

Joe held the bit of broken pottery. "I started thinking about buried treasure," he said. "But instead of pirate chests, I imagined big clay pots full of gold."

Fenton Hardy marveled at his younger son. "You could be right," he said. "I was so caught up in conventional detective reasoning, I refused to see other possibilities. An investigator's most valuable tool is his imagination, and I wasn't using mine. The broken piece of pottery may be an accidental clue, not to a smuggling scheme, but to something else."

The Hardys and Nancy agreed to make a thorough search of the small village. Next morning, they spread out to interview as many people as they could. In the afternoon, they compared notes.

"The only thing everyone agrees on is that there is supposed to be a hidden treasure around here," Nancy said.

"And that one person in town knows something about the treasure, but he's not telling anyone," Joe said. "That man is Pedro Lopez."

Fenton Hardy nodded. "We should pay a visit to Señor Lopez."

Turn to page 106.

"We have to act fast," Joe said. "He'll make such a ruckus that the other guy will hear."

"What do you have in mind?" Nancy asked.

"Let's go inside and overpower the smuggler. But we'll have to surprise him so he won't have time to reach for a weapon."

"He values possessions more than people," Nancy said. "I think we can catch him by playing on his selfish greed without even lifting a finger!"

She raced into the room with Joe right behind her. The man at the desk stared at them for a moment, not comprehending what was going on. In a flash, Nancy grabbed the beautiful serpent figure and held it high over her head.

"If you make one false move," she said, "I'll smash this into a million pieces!"

The man shrieked. "Oh, please, don't!" he pleaded. "It's the only one of its kind in the world!"

Nancy had no intention of destroying the priceless artifact. But her threat held the man motionless. He confessed everything.

"The man you met at the airport is my accomplice. He works for Salazar. He told you that Fenton Hardy wanted you to stop the investigation. He didn't realize you couldn't be tricked so easily. This was going to be our last job. But now we'll all go to jail."

Turn to the next page.

"That's right," Joe said. "My dad will be happy to hear the name of your other accomplice in Mexico, which you'd better tell us. The police will be just as pleased to pick up your friend in the cellar. My brother, Frank, already went after the man who professed to be Salazar."

A telegram to Mexico City and a phone call to the police brought a sudden end to the case. Salazar's company was above suspicion, and the three sleuths were available as detectives once more, the work they liked more than anything else in the world.

END

Joe beamed a staccato shaft of reflected sunlight from his signal mirror at Frank. *The man we followed is watching you. Nancy and I will distract him. Come running in exactly three minutes,* the message said.

Nancy punched the second hand on her stop watch when she saw Frank glance at his. "He's got it," she said.

Nancy and Joe sneaked behind Enrico Salazar, who didn't know they were there and who waited for Frank and Ernesto to approach him. The smuggler reached into his pocket for a weapon.

"Now!" Nancy yelled.

Enrico spun around, startled by her loud shout. He was caught off guard as Joe tackled him around the legs at the same instant that Frank grabbed him around the waist. The stunned smuggler went down without a struggle.

A short time later, the New York City police arrived and took away the prisoner. Enrico Salazar's smuggling scheme was over.

END

The Salazar Importing Company office was in the front part of a large warehouse in a rundown area of Manhattan. The investigators observed the building from a safe distance.

"By the looks of things, they're not doing much business," Nancy said. "The place seems virtually abandoned."

As she spoke, a truck pulled up behind the warehouse. A man got out and disappeared inside but soon came back carrying a large cardboard box stuffed with papers.

"What's he doing?" Joe asked.

"Those look like files," Nancy said. "I'm going to check at the office in front."

"Be careful," Joe said as Nancy vanished around the corner.

"Something tells me we should all be careful," Frank warned.

Turn to page 107.

"Let me speak to Drake," he said.

"This is Drake," a man replied.

"This so-called Feathered Serpent you sold me is a fake," Joe said in a muffled voice. "I want my money back. I'm sending a messenger over right now." He hung up before the surprised Drake could respond, and turned to Chet. "You're going to be our messenger."

Chet gulped. "I should have stayed underwater!"

A short time later, he entered the Salazar office. A stocky man eyed him with suspicion. "You from the Byron Gallery?" he asked. Chet mumbled that he was. The man jabbed a gun into Chet's ribs. "No, you ain't," he said. "I called Mr. Byron and he didn't know anything about a messenger. You're with the Hardys. Now take me to them, or else!"

Turn to page 110.

Pedro Lopez did not want to talk with the investigators and would not allow them into his small blacksmith shop. While the Hardys distracted him, Nancy sneaked around in back of the building.

She found a mound of broken bits of very old pottery and studied them with her magnifying glass. The break lines indicated the pots had been whole until very recently. They were storage jars, I'm certain, Nancy mused. She looked closely at the inside surface of a shard. Telltale circular lines were impressed in ancient dust on the clay. These were made from coins, Nancy thought. Señor Lopez found the buried treasure hidden in these pots!

She quickly joined the others and confronted the blacksmith. "Señor Lopez, I'd like to see what kind of metal you work with," she said.

"I only work with iron," the man told her.

Nancy stared at him accusingly. "And what kind of metal do you *melt*?" she asked pointedly. "*Gold?*"

Turn to page 109.

Nancy casually walked alongside the Salazar Importing Company building. A sign at the office door caught her eye: CLOSED FOR VACATION. She peered in the window, but no one was in sight.

Suddenly a man grabbed her by the arm. "What are you doing here?" he demanded.

"I, er, I was looking for a job and—" She didn't have time to finish her sentence because the man was not about to be fooled.

"You're Nancy Drew," he cried in astonishment. "You are supposed to be on your way to Mexico City . . . ." he stopped when he realized he was giving himself away.

Nancy had to think fast. "I didn't go," she said. "Frank and Joe Hardy left on the noon plane, Mr. Salazar. They asked me to check into the smuggling operation on this end."

"How do you know I am Salazar?" the man grunted.

"You're the only one who knows I came to investigate the case with the Hardys," Nancy said. "*Your* case!"

Salazar pulled her into the building through the front door. "Well, for you the case is over," he hissed. "And tonight, *everything* for you will be over!"

Turn to the next page.

He tied Nancy up and carried her into the warehouse. The huge room was filled with large wooden shipping crates. Many were covered with dust. "What are you going to do with me?" Nancy asked.

"You will know the answer to that tonight," Salazar said with a fiendish chuckle, "when I torch this building and all this unsold merchandise."

"You set up this whole scheme to cover up arson," Nancy exclaimed. "There is no smuggling operation. Your business is failing. Some of these crates have been here for months, I can tell. You thought you'd collect the insurance."

"Not *thought*, Miss Drew. I will!" Salazar said. "And I have a perfect alibi. It was the *smugglers* who did it, you see. And the best-known detective in the world will confirm that he was investigating smugglers in my company."

"Very clever," Nancy said. "You even removed your files so the insurance people won't be able to find any records that show you're going broke."

"You are clever, Miss Drew," Salazar said. "It is too bad you are not on the plane with your friends. I should have insisted in the fake phone call from Fenton Hardy that all three of you go to Mexico City. But never mind. It doesn't matter now."

Turn to page 119.

Señor Lopez began to quiver as a result of her shrewd questioning. He nodded quietly. "Yes," he said.

"You found the treasure of Contadero, didn't you?" Nancy went on. Again the man nodded and confessed what he had done. He had found the fabled gold, but if he had announced his find, the government would have claimed it as a national treasure. So he had melted the coins and gold pieces.

"But what connection is there with Salazar?" Fenton Hardy asked. "How did the broken piece of pottery get into a packing crate shipped to his warehouse in New York City?"

Nancy smiled, "That is another mystery," she said. "But I think I have the answer."

Turn to page 115.

When Chet, with his hands up, walked to where the Hardys and Nancy were waiting, the young investigators knew their plan had backfired. It had smoked out the smuggler, but at the risk of Chet's life! Rather than take any more chances, they, too, raised their arms.

"You kids figured you could outsmart me, eh?" Drake said with a smug grin. "Well, you're all going for a ride to the city dump." As he spoke, the big garbage truck the young people had seen the previous night roared around the corner. "Got any last words?" Drake chuckled.

"Yes," Frank said solemnly. "I'd like to say something to my good friends."

"You can talk on the way to the dump in the back of that truck," Drake snarled. "Now get going."

"Those aren't the friends I meant," Frank said. "Those are." He pointed to a New York City police squad car rounding the corner. Three more appeared as if from nowhere.

"The cops!" Chet cried out in delight. "How—"

"I called them when you went into the office," Frank said. "Luckily there was a phone booth nearby."

As Drake was hauled off by the officers, the young detectives smiled with satisfaction. "Boy," Chet said to Frank, "I'm glad your 'friends' made it here in time. I wasn't looking forward to going to the city dump!"

END

"That made you suspicious, right?" Frank asked.

"Yes," Mr. Hardy said. "So I pretended to go to Mexico City, but instead I followed him back to the warehouse. However, he discovered me and knocked me out. I'm afraid he took the smuggled goods and got away."

"Not quite," Frank said. "You see, after he got rid of you, he came to Bayport to scare us off the case. But it didn't work. We followed him back here. He must have changed his shirt and grabbed the loot, then left. Nancy and Joe went after him. Let's call the police!"

In minutes, the two Hardys were racing through the streets of New York City in a sleek blue-and-white police cruiser. At the wheel was Sergeant Barney Rourke.

"Our helicopter unit has your yellow sedan in sight now, Frank," the police officer said as he steered the car through heavy traffic, its siren wailing. "In fact, there's the copter now."

"And there's our car," Frank shouted. "And right in front is Ernesto Salazar!"

Fenton Hardy rubbed his sore head. "I'd like to be the first to greet him." The police car cut in front of the suspect, and the famous detective leaped out of the car as soon as it stopped.

Sergeant Rourke joined Mr. Hardy, who captured the surprised smuggler. Frank, Nancy, and Joe watched with pride as the curious case came to an end.

END

With that, he pushed Chet overboard. "I can't swim!" Chet screamed. "I can't swim . . . ." Slowly he sank out of sight.

"And now, the rest of you," Sergio commanded.

The investigators stepped off the boat. They bobbed and flailed in the waves next to the *Sleuth.* "You're not going to get away with this," Nancy cried out.

The man laughed as he and his henchman watched the three youths drifting away. "Oh, yes I will. Salazar has no idea that his own brother-in-law is using the company to smuggle precious artifacts from Mexico. When Fenton Hardy hears you're all lost at sea, he'll drop the investigation. By the time anyone picks it up again, I'll have millions and will be long gone."

His accomplice began to grow impatient. "Your chubby friend was most helpful," he said to Nancy and the Hardys. "He went straight to the bottom without a fuss. Now if you'd all be so kind as to join him . . . ."

As the two criminals leaned over the side of the *Sleuth* to watch the young people gasping for what seemed to be their last breath, Chet Morton slipped over the opposite side of the boat and bounded across the deck. His broad shoulders struck both men and pitched them into the sea.

Turn to page 114.

Then he made a powerful swan dive toward the spot where his friends struggled to stay above water, and with his pocket knife, freed their hands. With a few strong strokes, the three detectives swam to the startled kidnappers and subdued them. Soon everyone was aboard the *Sleuth* again, but this time the two men were tied and the four friends were free to enjoy the ride back to Bayport.

"You were right, Nancy," Chet said with a satisfied grin.

"About what?" Nancy asked.

"About diving alone. I promised I'd never do it again. And I didn't." He nodded toward the soaking-wet prisoners shivering at the back of the speeding boat. "I want to thank both of you for joining me," he said with a laugh.

END

Nancy led the curious band of investigators up the street of Contadero after the police had arrested Señor Lopez for not revealing his discovery. They stopped in front of a small building. The sounds of hammering filled the air. They entered a workshop stacked high with wooden packing crates. A carpenter was busily making more in the rear.

"This is Señor Garcia," Nancy said. "I interviewed him earlier. He makes the packing crates used to ship Salazar's goods to the United States. Watch him."

The investigators looked at the man work. As he finished a crate, he placed a clay pot in it and dropped the whole thing onto the hard floor. The pot did not break and the man smiled with satisfaction.

"Where do you get the pots to test your crates?" Nancy asked after she had introduced the others and explained what they were looking for.

"Now I must buy them," the man said. "But for many months I got old pots from Señor Lopez, the blacksmith. He had many."

The Hardys and Nancy flew back to the United States content and relaxed. It had been a most curious case indeed.

END

When Enrico Salazar saw the flashing light, he realized he was surrounded. He raced to a trapdoor in the floor of the rotting pier concealing a hidden stairway and disappeared. Seconds later the explosive roar of an engine echoed through the rickety building.

"He's got a boat down there!" Frank exclaimed as he rushed to the hidden steps. "Ernesto! Tell the police to send a boat. Joe! Nancy! Come with me!"

The three sleuths clattered down the stairs in time to see Enrico Salazar's boat pull away from its hiding place. Soon it would be in the open river, but first it had to navigate around the pilings supporting the pier.

Frank leaped onto the sleek motorboat. "Give yourself up," he shouted as the craft weaved around the thick poles.

"I planned this smuggling scheme too long to give it up so easily," Enrico Salazar answered defiantly. He cut the throttle, slowing the boat to a crawl. "Once you're out of the way, I'll be gone and the cops'll never find me!"

Turn to the next page.

Frank quickly sized up the dangerous predicament in which he found himself. The man was clearly desperate and would try anything to escape. As Salazar approached him, Frank kicked the boat's throttle wide open. The powerful engines roared to life again, thrusting the craft forward with a sudden leap. Frank jumped overboard but Salazar, surprised by the sudden lurch, tumbled to the deck. The boat picked up speed and then, driverless, plowed head-long into a thick black piling, smashing the hull in an eruption of water and noise.

Frank swam to Salazar and dragged the stunned smuggler to the foot of the steps where Nancy and Joe helped both of them out of the water.

The hum of a New York City police boat signaled the end of the case for the young detectives, who watched as a saddened Ernesto Salazar offered his hand to his brother as the police took Enrico away. "Perhaps he can be helped somehow," Nancy said.

"We hope so," Frank and Joe Hardy said in unison, because they knew the importance of having a brother to be proud of.

END

"You stay here while I circle around your brother," Frank said to Ernesto Salazar. "When I whistle, you make a lot of noise and I'll . . ."

The expression on Ernesto Salazar's face suddenly turned grim. He was no longer friendly, but evil. "You kids are too smart for your own good," he hissed. "My brother and I had a perfect smuggling operation going until our bookkeeper discovered it. *He* hired your father to investigate, not me."

Frank's mind was spinning. "So you decided to *pretend* to help the investigation," he said. "You faked being knocked out by your brother so you could get the three of us to this abandoned pier. The whole plan from the note on our car at the airport to now has been a trick so you could get rid of us."

Salazar grinned devilishly. "Exactly," he snarled. "And you've played right into our hands. As soon as Enrico brings your brother and Nancy Drew here, you'll all have a chance to say good-bye."

Frank shuddered. They'd been lured into a devious, well-planned trap. It could be their last.

Turn to page 120.

Late that night the steets and alleys in lower Manhattan were pitch dark. A lone figure crept through the shadows and paused near the rear entrance to the importing company. A spark flickered. Soon a bright flame leaped from the end of a torch held by a man. It was Salazar! He approached a side window and smashed it with his elbow. Then he raised the torch to throw it inside when suddenly the entire area exploded with light. Dozens of New York City policemen with brilliant searchlights pinned the dishonest importer at the end of their inquisitive beams.

"Don't throw it, Salazar," a booming voice called out. "It's all over."

Nancy, Joe, and Frank stepped from the shadows as Salazar was taken away.

"I'm glad Salazar believed that you were on that plane to Mexico," Nancy said. "If he had come looking for you and caught you, too—"

"We couldn't have rescued you," Joe finished. "But don't worry, we did. Case closed."

END

The creak of footsteps on the rotting pier timbers warned him that Enrico Salazar was nearby, and the gruff sound of the man's voice told him Enrico had already captured Joe and Nancy. Unless Frank could think of something immediately, all three investigators would be doomed. His eyes fell to the rickety boards beneath Ernesto's feet. The floor where they stood was as rotten as wet cardboard.

I've got to risk it, Frank thought. He leaped high into the air to land heavily on the weakened wood with all his weight. The planks snapped and both Frank and the startled smuggler dropped into the cold water below!

"Save my brother!" Enrico Salazar screamed from where he stood with Joe and Nancy. "He can't swim!" Joe and Nancy saw their chance as the terrified man stood helplessly watching his brother sink underwater. They grabbed Enrico and took him prisoner, while Frank scooped Ernesto in his arms and swam to the safety of a rickety stairway leading up to the pier.

As Frank and Joe guarded their captives, Nancy called the New York City police, and soon the criminals were on their way to jail. After sending a telegram to Fenton Hardy in Mexico telling him of the strange twist to the smuggling scheme, the case was officially closed.

END

"Did my father ask what time our plane would arrive?" Frank asked the agent.

"Why, yes," the man said. "I told him it would take about five hours and he said, good, he was just having lunch, which meant he'd see you around supper time."

The three investigators put their heads together after they left the counter. "Now *I'm* suspicious," Nancy said. "It's twelve noon here. Mexico City time is two hours earlier. Do you really think your father would be having *lunch* at ten o'clock in the morning?"

"Whoever made the call forgot about the time change. Obviously he was calling from this area!" Frank said.

"Someone wants to get us out of town awfully bad," Joe added.

"The only person who knows that Dad's in Mexico besides us, Mom, and Aunt Gertrude is Mr. Salazar," Frank pointed out.

"I think this calls for a visit to his office in New York," Nancy said, and went outside with the Hardys to their car.

Turn to page 104.

The trio rushed across the street. They saw the man hailing a taxi and noticed that the package under his arm was marked SALAZAR IMPORTING COMPANY.

The young investigators got into a different cab and ordered the driver to follow the suspect. He led them to a swank apartment building at Fifth Avenue and Eighty-first Street.

There the young people ran into an obstacle. The doorman would not let them enter. "You can't come in here unless someone's expecting you," he said.

Suddenly a muffled female voice could be heard over the building's intercom. "It's all right, Alfred. They can come up."

The young detectives stared at one another in disbelief.

"Who—" Frank started to blurt out, but Nancy put her finger to her lips.

"Dolores," she whispered. "Dolores *Guzman!*"

Turn to page 77.